For Jody, Sophie, and Milo—nearly flawless

Also by Berkeley Breathed:
Edwurd Fudwupper Fibbed Big
The Last Basselope
Red Ranger Came Calling
Goodnight Opus
A Wish for Wings That Work

First Edition

LCCN 2003104561

10 9 8 7 6 5 4 3 2 1

IM

Printed in Singapore

The illustrations for this book were done in acrylic on watercolor paper.
The text was set in Optima.

FLAWED DOGS

The 2004 Catalogue of the PIDDLETON DOG POUND's Very Available Leftovers

Unpolished Gems! One-of-a-Kind Finds!

∽ SOME MINOR BLEMISHES ∽

PRESENTED FOR YOUR CONSIDERATION BY HEIDY STRÜDELBERG:
PROPRIETOR, PIDDLETON DOG POUND

*Illustrated, photographed, and described by Berkeley Breathed
and the Friends of the Piddleton Pound*

LITTLE, BROWN AND COMPANY
New York ∽ An AOL Time Warner Company

Piddleton, Vermont
Pop. 327
(People: 243)

ACKNOWLEDGMENTS

Jeezum Crow! Compiling this year's Leftovers Catalogue for Heidy Strüdelberg has seen a super-D-duper effort on everyone's part!

First off, new summer resident Berkel Brethed was a blue ribbon dear for contributing his bright and colorful hand-painted pooch portraits. We're not sure what he used to do, but clearly Berkel should be encouraged in the arts. Idleness in one's autumn years is the devil's playground!

Thank you and a big squooshy bearhug to my sweet husband, Burton, who photographed and personally printed all the black & white photos in our bathroom. "None of that digital piffle for me!" Burton likes to say quite often.

Adding a spiritual angle to the project was my idea this year, and the members of Piddleton's Poetry Club—I'm president!—composed a sensitive verse for each dog's page. Pictured is me on the left, then Emily Flossbottom, Bubber Tinkle III (of the Burlington Tinkles), and Frieda "Freebird" Fillerup. Bubber wanted me to mention that he wrote the limericks while off his medication, when he's much funnier.

And finally, a big wet hound dog facelick for Laurence "K-9" Kirshbaum, CEO of AOL Time Warner Book Group. His generous financial advance allowed us to pay Heidy's bail after her arrest following last winter's Midnight Neuter Raids on the puppy mill breeders across town. Officially, we know nothing about any of that and—Good Lord 'n' butter!—we haven't a clue as to who detached the champion pit bull's bits!

Tammy Quackenbush

Tammy Quackenbush
President, Friends of the Piddleton Pound
President, Piddleton Poetry Club
President, Vermont Booster Broads
Vice President, Vegetarian Quilters against Land Mines and Bazookas
Treasurer, Chicken Liberation Front

THE SECRETS OF HEIDY STRÜDELBERG

Heidy asked me to write a bit about her, so she wouldn't have to. Easier asked than done. Honestly. She's at once the Garbo, Joan of Arc, and Mother Teresa of the nation's unwanted dogs: a reclusive warrior-saint of poundpups.

How'd she get this way? I Googled her and got this: Heidy emerged as an orphan from the ruins of post-war eastern Europe and emigrated to these shores at thirteen. She was swept up with the boom in specialized vanity dog breeding and became wealthy developing a superior, hairless strain of Bombay Peahound. She eventually became president of the American Kennel Club and spent a decade as the celebrated chief judge of the Westminster Dog Show.

Then 1994 happened.

As Heidy was entering the front doors of Madison Square Garden to judge that year's Westminster Best-in-Show Award, she encountered a shivering three-legged streetdog she later named Sam the Lion (pictured on page 34). A faded ear tattoo suggested a past life in a research lab. Witnesses remember that Sam licked her chin and lay his head in the warmth of her cupped hand. And then—still standing on his three remaining feet—he fell asleep.

We still don't know exactly what the spark was, but the fuse to Heidy's inner powder keg had been lit.

Minutes later in the dog show, the spotlight found Heidy holding up Sam the Lion—dripping mud and still snoring—with the Best in Show ribbon attached to his ragged collar.

You'll recall that the well-dressed mob then tore out most of the Garden's seats before the fire hoses restored order. Heidy retired from the professional dog world that afternoon and retreated to the Vermont mountains, buying a crumbling grain elevator and transforming it into the Last Chance Dog Pound—a refuge of hope where the doomed and most desperate are sent from other shelters around the country for a final try at getting adopted into a world that worships perfection.

Welcome to Heidy's World. Choose wisely.

Berkeley Breathed

Berkeley Breathed
Piddleton, Vermont
October, 2003

Dog Show Riot

Westminster judge declares 3-legged street dog Best-in-Show. Police move in.

In a dramatic move still unexplained, Westminster judge Heidy Strüdelberg suddenly interrupted the final judging by running to the street outside Madison Sqaure

The crowd exploded with fury as Strüdelberg pinned the blue ribbon upon the shabby dog's collar. As she was wrestled to the ground by Westminster officials, she was heard to cry out "Not for the cut of their coat, but for the content of their character shall we love them!"

Police in riot gear arrived in minutes and turned fire hoses upon the hysterical mob while over 200 show dogs ran amuck into

BOWSER BOOST

Enter Heidy's Gallery of Champions for 2004.

Please watch where you step.

Bipsie

Bipsie was bought to replace

The dearly departed Sweetface.

A beauty in blues

With some parts chartreuse

She clashed with the whole bloody place.

Noodles

Noodles never understood
The line his tongue was crossing
When he roamed the neighborhood
And did his mental flossing.

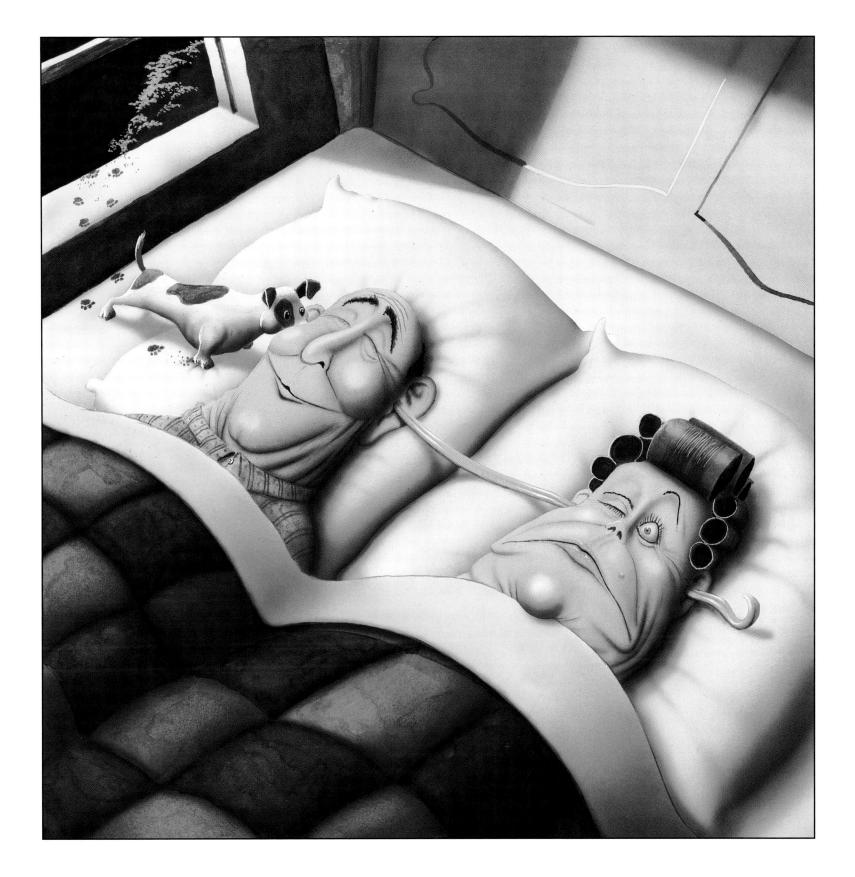

TINA

If Tina were a rhinoceros

She wouldn't seem so preposterous,

But then she ain't.

Hence, the complaint.

Lulu

Lulu was no looker,

An awkward nightingale.

To the pound they took her.

Accessorizing failed.

Rollo

Sister Sue was slow to see
The spots on gentle Rollo.
But after Bishop noticed he,
Sister strolled on solo.

Titus

Titus was a birthday gift
From Bubba's momma Wenti.
Bubba wanted a bulldog mix
And got one mixed aplenty.

Jeeve 5

Flimsy Jill Gawkie

Picked Jeeves for his jowls.

Then moved to Milwaukee

Where winds always howl.

One day on a walkie

She threw in the towel.

Pete

The Bibbles found
   They could no longer quibble,
The problem with Pete
   Went past iffy kibble.

Pepe

Pepe has set his crossed eyes

On winning a dog show grand prize.

   He looks in the mirrors

   And glamour appears

He'll win when a pig up and flies.

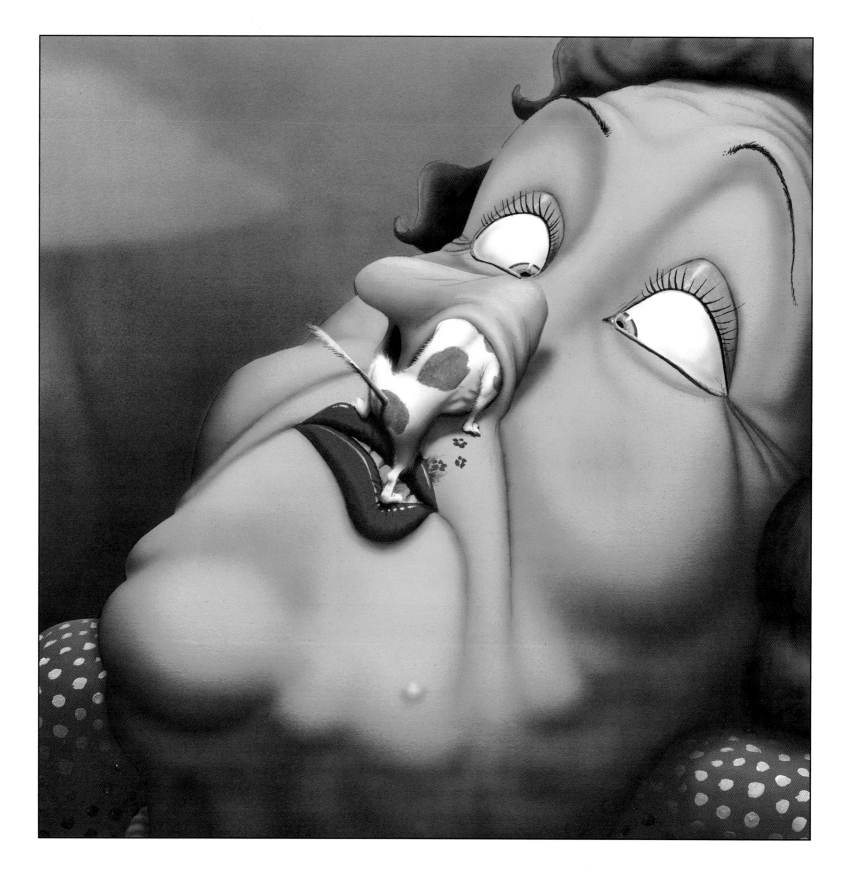

WILLY WONKER

A pup we'll call Willy Wonker

Was left by Helen from Yonker.

For size he's middlin'

But loves his nibblin'

He could not resist Helen's honker.

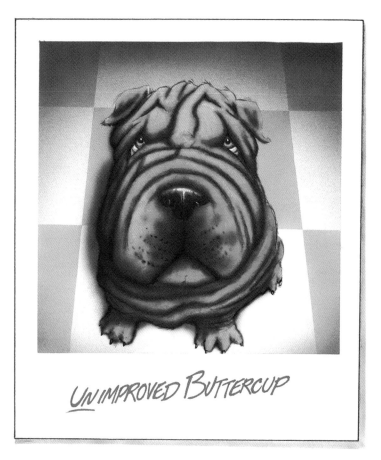

Unimproved Buttercup

Buttercup

Before Babs went to Heaven
She got tightened up.
Nips 'n' tucks counting seven,
Same for Buttercup.

Heather

Meet Heather with plenty of hair.

She figures it better than bare.

  Miss Pott kicked her out

  For she had a doubt

Whether any of Heather was there.

iBoo™

iBoo™ came completely loaded.

A perfect pet—with plug!

But out the box he downloaded

Right there upon the rug.

Ben

The Finns wanted twins

But got only Macken.

So in came in dear Ben

Whose looks were found lackin'.

A flop as Finn kin,

Poor Ben was sent packin'.

Sal

Here's Sal, it seems no one wants her.

Her ends will stroll off and wander.

  A long doggie weenie

  Of noisy linguine

Sal barks at her butt way down yonder.

BARNEY

Barney's pal had lived to autumn

When his years just up and caught 'im.

Now Barney wonders who would want 'im,

With Elvis Presley on his bottom.

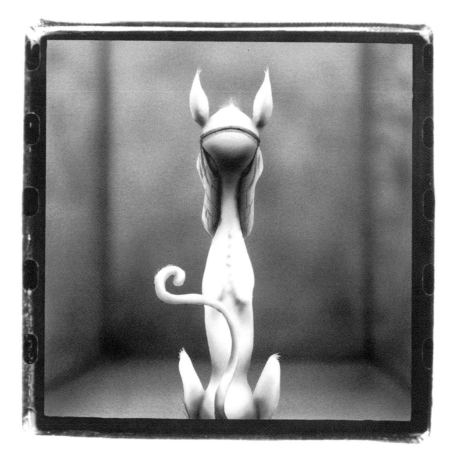

Spanks

There's something 'bout Spanks

That no one dismisses:

This dog don't bark

But quite often hisses.

Don't fetch no ball

But eats tunafishes.

We'll say it right here:

Something's amisses.

Sam the Lion

Sam the Lion: a mystery past,
A stray from east SoHo.
A refugee from research labs,
The rest we cannot know.

Except the day he rose to win
Westminster Best in Show!
One brief and golden moment, then—
They saw three paws below.

So in this world
Of the simple and odd,

The bent and plain,

The unbalanced bod,

The imperfect people

And differently pawed,

Some live without love...

That's how they're flawed.

To inquire about the possibility of adopting any of the anxious candidates described herein, contact Heidy Strüdelberg at FlawedDogs.com. If she hasn't a companion to suit you, please visit the souls who await you at your local shelter. Each year, more than 5 million animals—flawed no more than you and me—will have their lives ended unloved and alone.